SEA
SONGS

MYRA COHN LIVINGSTON, POET

LEONARD EVERETT FISHER, PAINTER

HOLIDAY HOUSE/NEW YORK

This book was set in Electra Bold type by American–Stratford Graphic Services, Inc. Color separations were made by Offset Separations Corp. It was printed on Moistrite Matte by Rae Publishing Co., Inc., and bound by The Maple-Vail Book Manufacturing Group. Typography by David Rogers.

The art was prepared with acrylic paint, the same size as it appears in the book. The pictures were created on a textured paper and then peeled from the back of the paper in preparation for laser light scanning.

Library of Congress Cataloging-in-Publication Data

Livingston, Myra Cohn.
Sea songs.

SUMMARY: Poetic images of cresting waves, mermaids, sunken ships, and other aspects of the sea.
1. Sea poetry, American—Juvenile poetry. 2. Children's poetry, American. [1. Ocean—Poetry.
2. American poetry] I. Fisher, Leonard Everett, ill.
II. Title.
PS3562.I945S4   1986   811'.54   85-16422
ISBN 0-8234-0591-5

SEA
SONGS

Crashing on dark shores, drowning, pounding
breaker swallows breaker. Tide follows
tide. Lost in her midnight witchery
moon watches, cresting tall waves, pushing
through mist and blackness the cold waters.

*Moon, you have worked long.
Now rest . . .*

Mermaids curl in coral beds. Kraken
wind long tentacles, weave tales of lost
sailors sleeping in beams of sunken
ships; tales of bright treasure buried in
silt and the glittering of doubloons.

Moon, you have gone mad.
Be still . . .

Caravels, lashed by tails of mermen
carry old dreams. Galleons, shouldered on
scaly arms, bound over the breakers.
Clouds gather in white mist. All is still.
Pale stars disappear in darkling sky.

*Moon, you speak in
strange riddles . . .*

Wind rises. Drizzle turns to raindrop.
Sea and sky split with thunder, gale howls.
Heaving ships, plunged into black waters,
vomit saltspray back to hissing seas,
sailing over, up and ever on.

Moon, you cry out with
nightmare . . .

This, Columbus saw beneath ocean
stretching from dark shores to wide, bright sands,
tossed and buffeted by strong iron
chains rusted with blood-red; yet never
waking from dream, he sailed in madness.

Moon, your tale is told.
Now sleep . . .

Drowned in foam, faded in the gray mist,
phantoms disappear. A sandpiper
prints the clean morning sand. Pelicans
plunge dive the whitecaps. Across distant
sea swells, sun gurgles, rising in light.

*Moon, your shadow
still watches . . .*

Fishermen unwind tangled nets, cast
trawls into marbled waters, snaring
schools of fish in their tarred, wet purses,
chumming and charming with live wriggling
anchovy and herring, a day's catch.

Sun, you watch behind
thin clouds.

Tilted umbrellas nod in soft sand.
Patchworks of bright towels sprawl beach picnics.
Surfboards ride the foaming surf. Painted
pails pour water into moated castles,
buried in the lost digs of summer.

*Sun, you climb higher
and higher.*

Ketches and sloops color the blue days.
Spinnakers of red rig for racing.
Dinghies and catamarans bobbing,
jumbles of masts and booms in dizzy
patterns, billow with walloping sails.

*Sun, you smile on
your play.*

Wind blows the water into furrows.
Waves leap toward the shore, the crests foaming
white, the whitecaps spraying, splaying,
dashing against pitted rocks, dying
slowly in the thirsty, sponging sands.

Sun, you sink as
you watch.

Under the sand, below the water
sun in spring feeds the floating plankton,
forking light on the drifting seaweeds,
multiplying herring, menhaden,
churning over the salts of the sea,

Sun, you bring life,
you bring food.

Cries of porpoise and dolphin echo
through dark submarine canyons and shelves.
Shrimp crackle, small croakers and drums hiss.
Huge rubber men pry from barnacles
giant scallops and swim with gray sharks.

*Here, sun, you can
still see.*

Deeper than this, dwell darkness and cold.
Sun cannot probe these underground dungeons
locked by sea devils and dragonfish,
flashing with light, turning on eerie
torches, kaleidoscopes of color.

No sun, no moon
sees here.

Who cries of what lies beyond, beneath
bottom realms? Volcanos rising from
ocean floor, golden with shells, gray wash
showered from earth, red clay, and wind dust?
Who speaks of mysterious red tides?

*Moon, you return
once more . . .*

LEE

Ghosts raise galley ships on crimson tides.
Sun flees. Foghorn cries to lighthouse.
Wind blows wild storms and over dark waves
mermaids sing bewitching sea songs to
sailors steering wildly toward the moon.

*Moon, speak once more
the dreams . . .*